Captain Flinn
and the
Pirate Dinosaurs
☠ Story Treasure Chest ☠

Written by Giles Andreae Illustrated by Russell Ayto

PUFFIN

PUFFIN BOOKS

Published by the Penguin Group: London, New York, Australia, Canada, India, Ireland, New Zealand and South Africa

Penguin Books Ltd, Registered Offices: 80 Strand, London WC2R 0RL, England

puffinbooks.com

Captain Flinn and the Pirate Dinosaurs first published 2005

Captain Flinn and the Pirate Dinosaurs: Missing Treasure! first published 2007

Captain Flinn and the Pirate Dinosaurs: The Magic Cutlass first published 2009

This collection published in Puffin Books 2010

004–10 9 8 7 6 5 4

CONTENTS

Captain Flinn
and the
Pirate Dinosaurs

For Flinn – G. A.
For my brother – R. A.

This is Flinn.
He is wearing his pirate T-shirt and
colouring in a picture he has drawn of a dinosaur.
Flinn LOVES dinosaurs.

One day at school, Flinn was colouring in a new
dinosaur picture when he realized he didn't have
quite enough pens.

"Why don't you have a look in the art cupboard, Flinn?"
said Miss Pie, his teacher. "I think there are
more colours at the back."

So Flinn opened the door
and stepped
into
the
cupboard.

There were lots of paints and rolls of paper and pots of glue, but Flinn couldn't see any pens.

As he searched, he heard a noise.

"Boohoo!
Boohoo hoo!
Boohoo!"

and then,

"Sniffle,
snuffle,
sniffle."

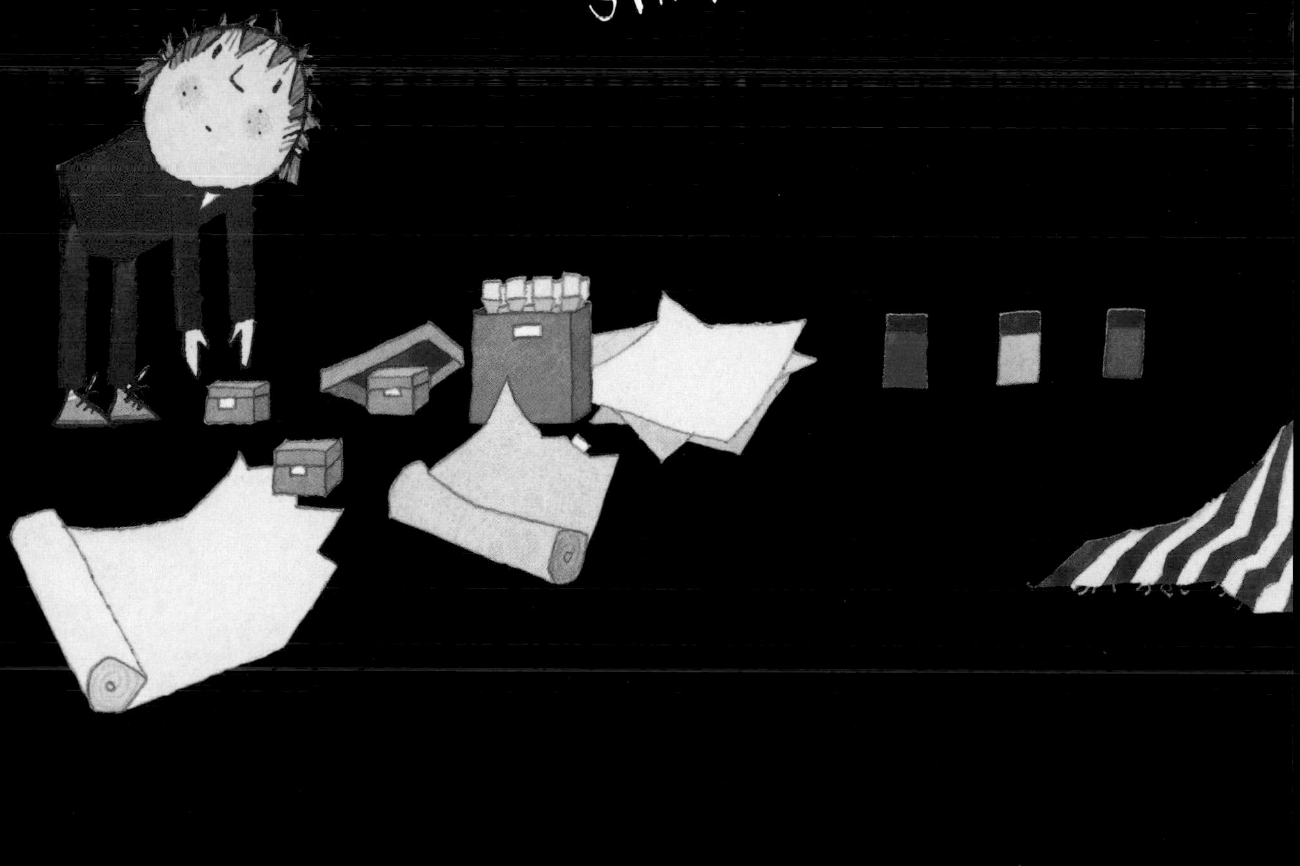

Right at the back of the cupboard,
under an old curtain, was something
shaking and **shuddering**
like a giant jelly.

Flinn crept closer and closer. When he
lifted up the curtain...

he couldn't believe his eyes!

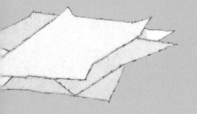

It was a real live
PIRATE CAPTAIN!

"Hello," said Flinn. "What's the matter?"

The pirate, whose name was Captain Stubble,
sniffed and looked at Flinn.

"My ship! They've stolen my ship!"
he sobbed. "One minute I was fast asleep and
the next I was in the water watching my
precious ship, the *Acorn*, sail away."

"But who has stolen it?" asked Flinn.

"I don't know," said Captain Stubble,
"but as I watched I heard a...

ROAR!

...And then a strange kind of song.

It went: 'Yo ho ho!
Yo ho ho!

Somethingy,
something –

Go! Go! Go!'"

"Hmmm, very strange," said Flinn. "How will you get your ship back?"

"I don't know," blustered Captain Stubble. "I can't do it on my own!"

"I could help," said Flinn bravely.

"And so will we!" It was Flinn's friends, Pearl, Tom and Violet.

"We love adventures!" they said.

And just at
that moment,
the back
of the cupboard
fell away and they all
tumbled out . . .

...into
    a bright
        blue
            day,

where an old pirate ship was waiting.
"She's not quite what I'm used to,"
said Captain Stubble, "but if this ship
helps me find my beloved *Acorn*,
then she'll do for me!

"All aboard!"

"Right, me hearties," said Captain Stubble, "if you're going to be pirates, you'll need to look like pirates."

Flinn brandished a gleaming silver cutlass.

"And since you seem to be so brave, Flinn," he said, "you can be Captain of this ship. I'd much rather be the cook."

So Captain Flinn took over

and they sailed . . .

...and sailed ... in search of the *Acorn.*

The pirates were about to give up hope, when
Pirate Violet shouted from the crow's-nest,

"SHIP AHOY!"

Stubble grabbed his telescope.
"That's my precious *Acorn*!" he cried.
"LET'S BOARD IT!" cried Captain Flinn.
"And reclaim your ship from those pirate
baddies! ALL HANDS ON DECK!"

They sailed faster and faster and got closer and closer.

When they were nearly alongside,
Captain Flinn put the telescope to
his eye. His face went white.
"They're not just ordinary pirates,"
he stammered, "they're...

"...PIRATE DINOSAURS!"

And that is exactly what they were.

There was a pirate diplodocus...

a pirate stegosaurus...

a pirate triceratops...

and a pirate pterodactyl!

And, right at the helm of the ship, steering its course with his claws on the wheel, was a GREAT...BIG...PIRATE...

...TYRANNOSAURUS REX!

When he saw
Captain Flinn he
roared an almighty

ROAR!

The dinosaurs sang out
in their terrible voices:

"Yo ho ho!
Yo ho ho!
Pirate
Dinosaurs
Go! Go! Go!"

"Attack!" cried Captain Flinn,
and a great battle began!
CLANG! CLASH!
SWISH! SPLASH!

It wasn't long before all the Pirate
Dinosaurs jumped overboard in terror.
All . . . EXCEPT . . .

...the Tyrannosaurus Rex! He roared an almighty

ROAR!

Captain Flinn could see his huge sharp yellow teeth, and his tonsils wobbling ferociously at the back of his throat.
"I challenge you to a duel!" shouted Captain Flinn.

"I'm going to cut you up into little pirate sausages!" yelled the Tyrannosaurus Rex, dribbling greedily. "Then I'm going to put you on the barbecue and

EAT YOU UP!

With much too much tomato ketchup!" he added.

"Oh no, you're not!" yelled Captain Flinn, and charged.
Their cutlasses FLASHED and CRASHED and BASHED and SMASHED

for at least two hours and twenty-five minutes until, **finally,**

the Tyrannosaurus Rex was **exhausted.**

"Captain Flinn," he stammered, "I surrender. You are such a great pirate that YOU should be the captain of all the Pirate Dinosaurs! Please spare me and I promise I'll be the goodest goody in the world. Honest!"

"Then maybe one day I will be your captain," replied Captain Flinn, "but now we'd better get back to school. It's almost lunchtime!"

So Captain Flinn took the wheel of the *Acorn*.
And while Pirate Pearl, Pirate Tom and Pirate Violet
untied the crew, Stubble made a delicious shark's-fin stew.

When they got to the harbour, they
waved goodbye to Captain Stubble
and to the Tyrannosaurus Rex.

Flinn saw that the door they had
fallen through was still hanging
open. So they all
              clambered in...

...and instantly they were back among
the paints and rolls of paper and pots of glue.
Flinn grabbed some colouring pens and
they all crept back into the classroom.

"And they all lived happily ever after," said Miss Pie, closing the book she had been reading. "You've been in that cupboard a long time, Flinn. What *have* you been doing?"

Flinn smiled secretly at his friends.

"Oh nothing," he said.
"Nothing really at all."

Captain Flinn
and the
Pirate Dinosaurs
~☠~
Missing Treasure!

For Ned – G.A.
For my mother and
father – R.A.

A note from the author:

"By the way, there is a dinosaur in this book called the **giganotosaurus**. It's a hard word, so it might be a good idea if you learn how to say it now. Take it bit by bit . . .

gig – an – OH – toe – SORE – us.

That's it!

Giganotosaurus!"

Why couldn't
the pirate play cards?

Because he was
sitting on the deck!

Flinn's board – KEEP OFF!

This is Flinn. Flinn LOVES dinosaurs.

Tomorrow is a very special day because Flinn's teacher, Miss Pie, is taking his class to see the dinosaur skeletons at the museum.

"Here we are!"
said Miss Pie.
"Now remember –
stay together and

don't

touch

anything!"

Flinn's class followed
the museum guide to
the Skeleton Room.

"Wow!" said Flinn to his
friends, Pearl, Tom and Violet.
"That one looks really *scary*."

"This is the giganotosaurus,"
said the guide.
"He was even **bigger**
and more **ferocious**
than the **mighty**
Tyrannosaurus Rex."

In the next room, there was a big glass case.
    But it was completely EMPTY!

"It used to hold the
treasure of the famous pirate
Captain Rufus Rumblebelly,"
explained the guide,
"but it was **stolen** last night!"

"Real pirate treasure?" said Flinn (who liked pirates
just as much as dinosaurs). "But **who** could have stolen it?"

"Look!" said Tom.
"Maybe these
peculiar feathers
are a clue . . ."

"They seem to be leading to
that cupboard," said Pearl.

"Let's follow them!"
said Violet.

So Flinn and his friends quietly opened
the door and slipped through.

PRIVATE

The cupboard was cold
and dark and full of
cobwebs.

"Wait a minute!"
said Flinn. "What's that?"

He bent down
and picked up a
gleaming golden coin.

"And look!
Here's another one."

"It must be the treasure!"
said Violet.

And just at that moment,
the back of the cupboard fell away
and Flinn and his friends
all
tumbled
out . . .

"What treasure?" asked Flinn,
as he quickly untied the pirate.

"Why, the famous treasure of
Rufus Rumblebelly!" said the pirate.
"I'm Gordon Gurgleguts and Rufus
Rumblebelly was my granddaddy.
I took the treasure from the museum –
just to have a little look – but then
someone stole it from **me!!**"

"That's **amazing!**" said Flinn.
"We're looking for the treasure too!
We'll help you find it,
but **only if** you promise
to take it **straight**
back to the museum."

"All right," said Gurgleguts.
"I promise."

"But who stole it?"
asked Flinn.
"I don't know," said Gurgleguts.
"But I did hear a strange song
as they sailed away.
It went:

'Yo ho ho!
Yo ho ho!
Bag o' Bones Island
Here we go!'"

"Then that's where **we'll** go!"
said Flinn. "To Bag o' Bones
Island! Come on, everyone!"
"Aye, aye!" said Gurgleguts.
"And why don't YOU be our captain?
Here – take my hat."

So Captain Flinn took the helm and they swiftly
set sail for Bag o' Bones Island.

"Island ahoy!" shouted
Pirate Violet from the crow's nest.

"Follow me, everyone,"
said Captain Flinn.
"There's thick jungle
ahead and we don't
want anyone to get lost . . ."

"Gurgleguts? Gurgleguts?"

"WHERE ARE YOU?"

"Wait," said Pirate Pearl.
"What's that noise?"

And don't think we've forgotten

That this pirate's rather

So let's bar

With some sp

"ROOOOAAARRRR!"

In front of them was a clearing. Captain Flinn peered into it and shuddered.
"Pirates!" he said. "But they're not just ordinary pirates. They're . . .

"...PIRATE DINOSAURS!"
And he was right!
There was . . .

A PIRATE DIPLODOCUS . . .

A PIRATE STEGOSAURUS . . .

A PIRATE TRICERATOPS . . .

AND A GREAT BIG PIRATE
TYRANNOSAURUS REX.

Beside the Pirate Dinosaurs
was a huge pile of gleaming
treasure. And next to the
treasure, tied up from head
to foot, was Gurgleguts.

The Pirate Dinosaurs were sin

"We've stolen all the tr

We'll use it

And won't it be a plea

For us all

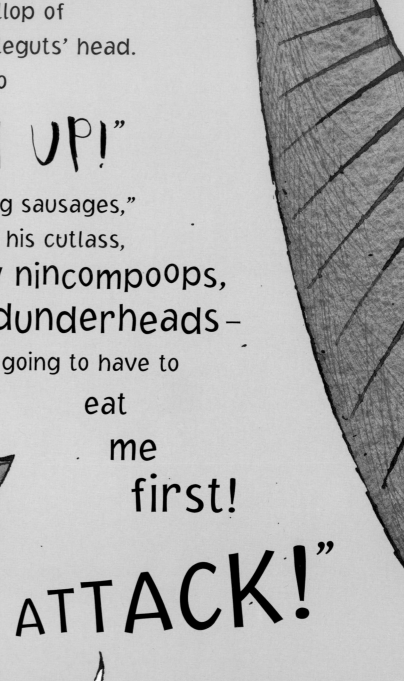

"Stop!" yelled Captain Flinn.
"Untie my friend **immediately!**"

"We couldn't possibly do that,"
said the Tyrannosaurus Rex,
squeezing a huge dollop of
tomato ketchup on to Gurgleguts' head.
"Because we're going to

EAT HIM UP!"

"Well then, you slimy seafaring sausages,"
said Captain Flinn, drawing his cutlass,
"you nasty *noodle-brained* nincompoops,
you dirty *dastardly* dunderheads –
you're going to have to

eat
me
first!

ATTACK!"

CRASH!

Suddenly, Captain Flinn took a huge
swipe at the Tyrannosaurus Rex,
and **pinned** him up against a tree.
"Please spare me,"
said the Tyrannosaurus Rex,
"and I promise to be
the goodest goody in the
whole world . . . EVER."

"You great **big fibber!**" said Captain Flinn.
"Fibber, eh?" said the Tyrannosaurus Rex angrily.
"Well then, I think it's time you met my cousin!"

The ground began to shake and an enormous shadow fell over the island.

There was the hugest, fiercest, most terrifying-looking dinosaur in the whole world.

"Gulp," said Captain Flinn. "Who are you?"

"I'M GIGANOTOSAURUS," roared the dinosaur, "and I'm so BIG and TOUGH and SCARY that nothing in the whole world ever frightens me!"

Then suddenly . . .

"Well, shiver me timbers," said Flinn.
"Fancy a big old dinosaur being
scared of a teeny-weeny spider!"

HHH!"

cried the Giganotosaurus.

"Spider! Spider!
Help! HEEEELP!!"

A tiny spider was hanging
from Captain Flinn's
pirate hat.

"They're just so creepy and crawly,"
wailed the Giganotosaurus.
"Keep him away
from me – please!"

In all the commotion,
Captain Flinn saw his chance.

He quickly freed Gurgleguts and,
in a flash, all the Pirate Dinosaurs AND
the Giganotosaurus were tightly tied up.

Then Captain Flinn picked up the treasure.
"Quick, gang," he said, "let's get back
to the ship. It's time to go home."
And off they all sailed.

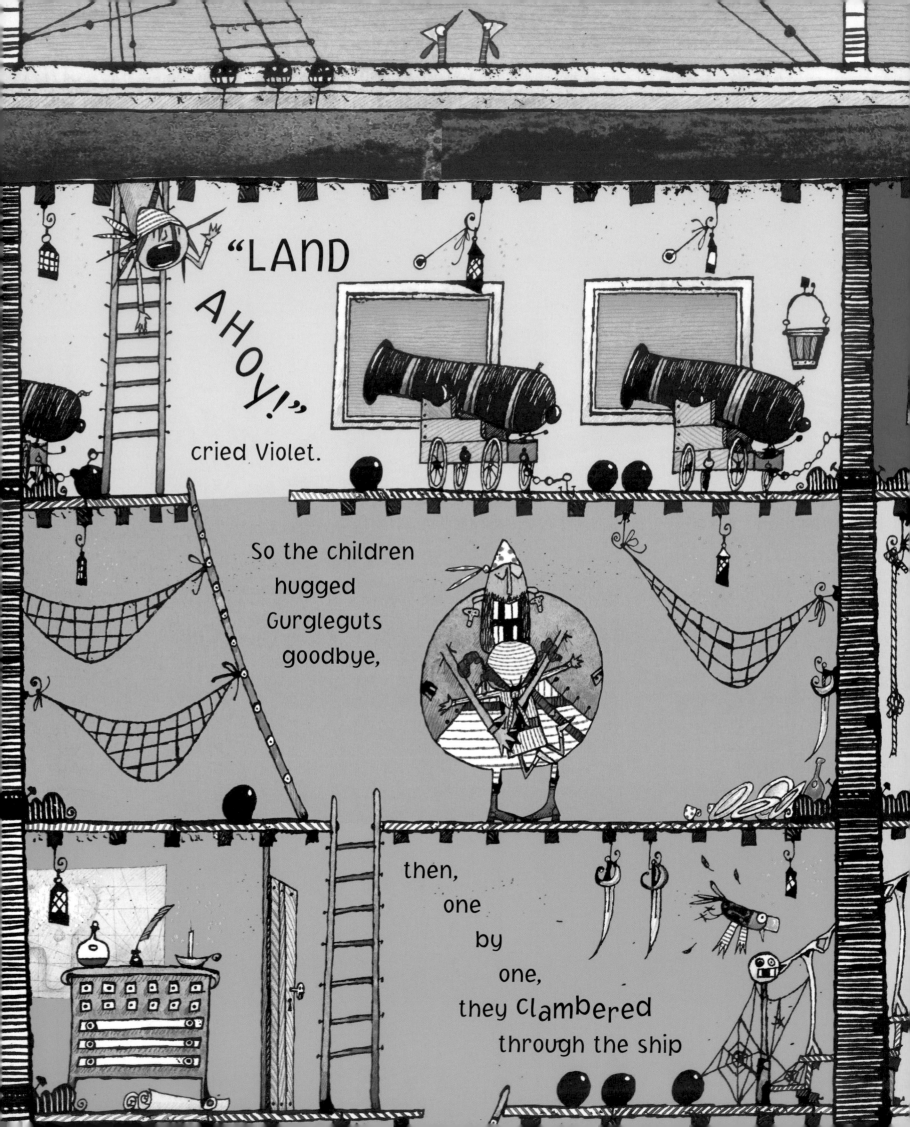

into the open cupboard . . .

. . . and back
into the museum.
"Wherever have you been?"
said Miss Pie.
"We've found the missing
treasure!" said Flinn.
"My goodness!" said the
museum guide. "Well done!
But WHO stole it?"

"It's a long story," said Flinn. "But it ended up in the hands of some pirates. Oh, and they weren't just pirates, they were PIRATE DINOSAURS!"

"Pirate Dinosaurs!" laughed the guide. "That's the silliest thing I've heard in my whole life! Pirate Dinosaurs indeed!"

"And just for your
information," added Flinn,
"I can tell you something
about your giganotosaurus.
He was **frightened** of **spiders**.
Very frightened indeed."

Captain Flinn
and the
Pirate Dinosaurs
The Magic Cutlass

For Rex – G.A.
To my brother – R.A.

It was the day of Flinn's school play.
Flinn was a Pirate Captain (Flinn LOVES pirates)
and his friends Pearl, Tom and Violet were the crew.

"Go on," said Miss Pie,
their teacher.
"It's your song now."

"I'm a pirate king
with a pirate ship.
And an ugly pirate crew,"
began Flinn . . .

when another voice boomed out,

"And if you don't all come with me I'll eat the lot of you!"

"My goodness, he looks scary," whispered one of the parents. "Do you think he's a new teacher or something?"

The scary
pirate with the
booming voice was
enormous.

He had a big red coat,
huge black boots and
very scaly green legs.

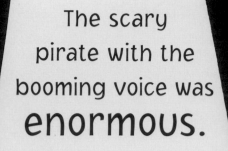

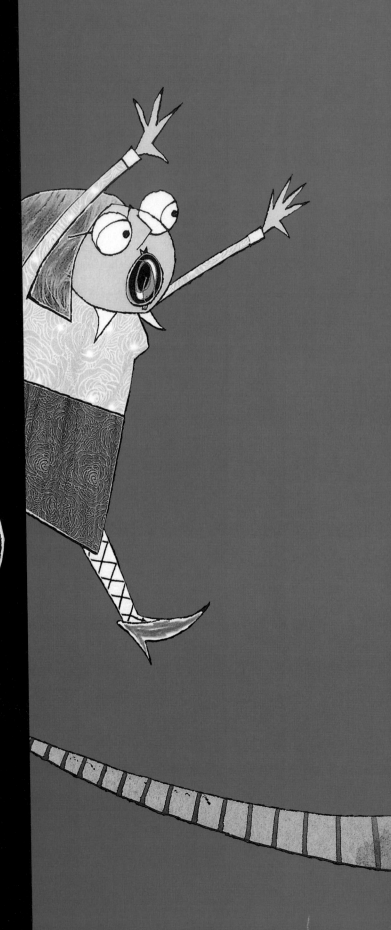

He grabbed Flinn and his friends and disappeared off the stage.
"No! No! That wasn't meant to happen," shrieked Miss Pie.
"Come back! COME BACK!!!"
But it was too late.
Uh-oh, thought Flinn. Here we go again!
The pirate threw a large blanket over Flinn and
his friends, and they felt themselves tumbling

down
through
the air
until . . .

They landed righl
on the main deck of an
old-fashioned pirate ship.

When they looked around,
they saw to their horror
that the pirates on
this ship were not
just ORDINARY pirates.

No, they weren't
ORDINARY pirates at all.
They were . . .

... PIRATE DINOSAURS!

There was

a Pirate Diplodocus,   a Pirate Stegosaurus,   a Pirate Triceratops,   a Pirate Pterodactyl

and, of course, their old arch-enemy . . .

the Pirate Tyrannosaurus Rex!

"Captain T. Rex," said Flinn.
"We meet again."

"Tie them up!"
yelled the Tyrannosaurus Rex.

"But leave this one to me. How delicious! What a treat! Blood and bones and scallywag meat!"

"Then why don't you just go and get it!" shouted Captain Flinn back.

The great big T. Rex looked shifty.

"Because, um . . . I can't swim," he muttered.

"Well, don't think I'm going to get it for you!" said Captain Flinn.

"Oh, but I think you will," said the Tyrannosaurus Rex, getting out his bottle of ketchup. "Because I'm feeling hungry and your little friends over there are looking tasty. VERY tasty indeed!"

"OK," said Captain Flinn angrily. "Then I guess YOU win."

So Pirate T. Rex and his fearsome crew,
and Captain Flinn and his captured mates sailed to sea.
It wasn't long before they reached
the exact spot. Then Captain Flinn dived down, down, down under
the sea, dodging sharks and giant octopuses

until, at last, he found the cutlass.

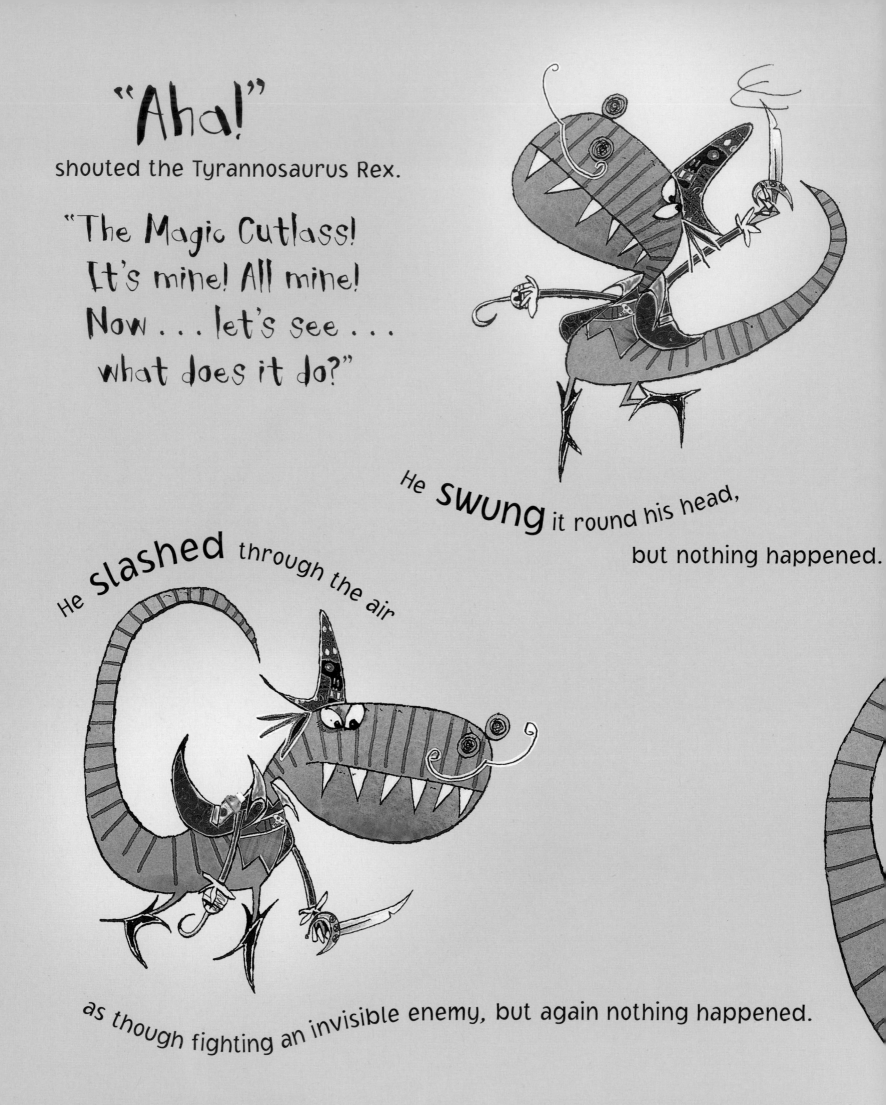

"Aha!"
shouted the Tyrannosaurus Rex.

"The Magic Cutlass!
It's mine! All mine!
Now . . . let's see . . .
what does it do?"

He SWUNG it round his head,

but nothing happened.

He slashed through the air

as though fighting an invisible enemy, but again nothing happened.

He danced a jig and looked very silly,

but still nothing happened.

"Bother, blast
and bellyache!"

roared the Tyrannosaurus Rex.

"This cutlass isn't magic at all.
It's blunt and rusty
and useless."

And he threw it away.

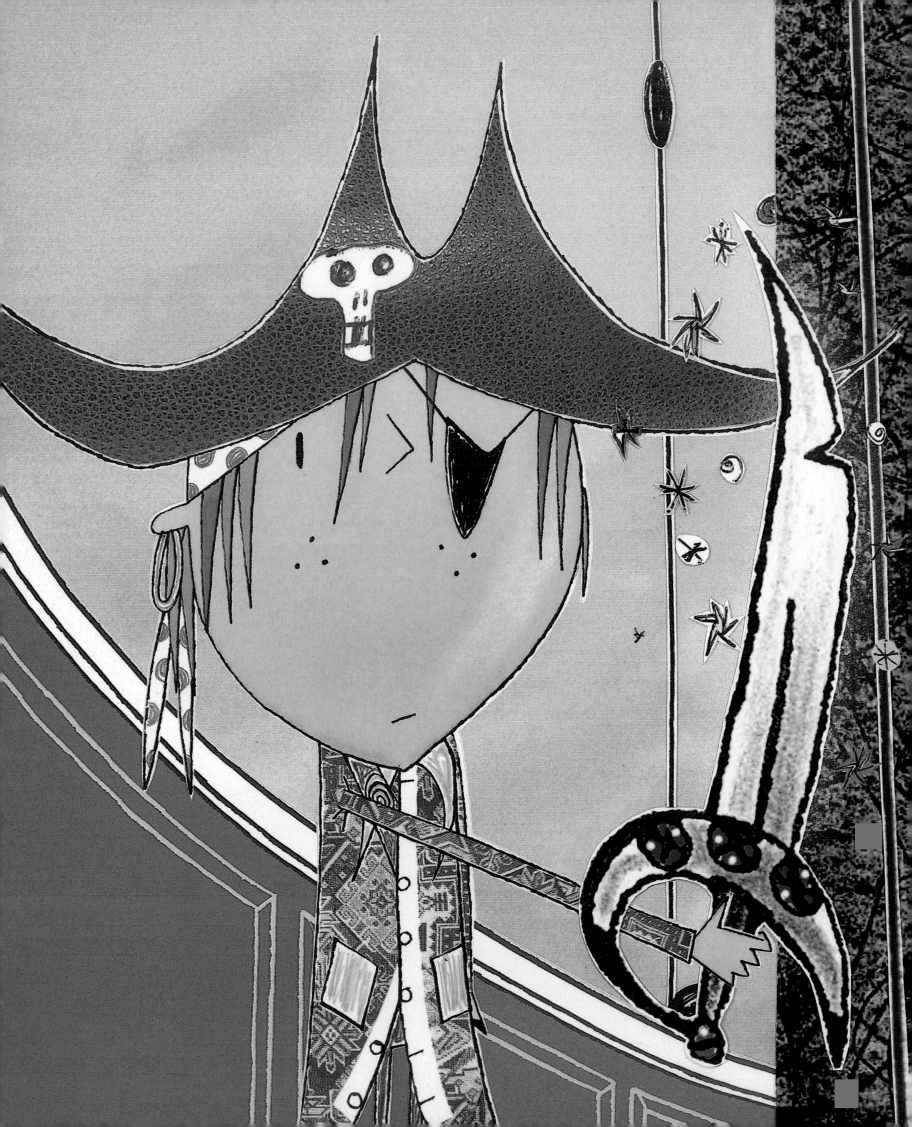

The cutlass
landed right beside
Flinn and he quickly picked it up.
"Oh, I wish I could untie these ropes," he said.

The cutlass began to *glow*
and suddenly the ropes round
Pearl, Tom and Violet fell
away

and his

friends

were free.

"That's it!" whispered Pirate Violet.

"That's the magic of the cutlass.

It grants wishes!"

Captain Flinn and his friends tried to sneak away,
but they were too late –
the Tyrannosaurus Rex
had spotted them.

"Not so fast!"

he roared,
snatching the cutlass back.

"I'm still hungry!"

"Well, you're not going to eat us, you great big fatso!" yelled Captain Flinn.

"Come on, gang – ATTACK!"

They swung from ropes and leapt from the rigging. Swords, cutlasses and daggers flew in every direction.

"Yo ho ho! Yo ho ho!" bellowed the Tyrannosaurus Rex.

SMASH!

CRASH!

The Pirate Dinosaurs were brave, but Captain Flinn and his crew were **even** braver and, after a long struggle, they finally had all the Pirate Dinosaurs safely tied up.

"Right-ho, matey," said Captain Flinn, marching the Tyrannosaurus Rex to the side of the ship. "Time to

walk the

plank!"

"But I can't swim!"
shrieked the Tyrannosaurus Rex.
His knees began to knock as he
looked down and saw sharks
circling beneath him.

"Help!" he yelled.
"I want my mummy!
Oh, I wish my mummy was here!"

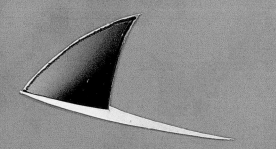

Suddenly, there was
a **great**
big
bang!
A huge **lady** Tyrannosaurus Rex appeared –
the cutlass had worked its magic AGAIN.

"Mummy??!!!!"

"What do you think you're doing?" bellowed the Mummy Tyrannosaurus Rex. "What did I say about only picking on people your own size? And how many times have I told you never to play with swords?"

"Um, sorry, Mummy," said the Tyrannosaurus Rex.

"What a naughty boy you are," said his mummy. *"Now, give that cutlass back to the little boy and play together nicely!"*

The Tyrannosaurus Rex grumpily handed the cutlass back to Captain Flinn. "Quick, gang," said Captain Flinn to his friends. "Hold on to the cutlass and say along with me, **'I wish we could go home!'"**

The cutlass began to *glow*

and suddenly Captain Flinn, Pearl, Tom and Violet

found themselves flying through
the air until they

landed with a bump

back on the stage at school.

"Right," said Captain Flinn.
"Um, sorry about that.
Now, where was I? Oh yes . . .

*I'm a pirate king with a pirate ship.
And an ugly pirate crew,"*
began Flinn, when Miss Pie appeared.
"Where on earth have you been?"
she demanded. "And what's that sword
thingy in your hand, Flinn?"

But Flinn didn't answer. He decided to use the magic cutlass
and make one last wish. Miss Pie would probably never have
believed him anyway and actually she did look rather good . . .